Time to Celebrate!

One morning, in school, Eddie said to his teacher, "February is the shortest month in the year, but it has the most celebrations."

"I guess you're right, Eddie," Mrs. Andrews said. "There are two important birthdays."

"Abraham Lincoln's and George Washington's," said Rodney.

"And Valentine's Day!" said Anna Patricia.

"And Groundhog Day," said Boodles.

"And there's Pickle Week!" said Eddie.

"There's Pencil Week, too," said Anna Patricia. "And Brotherhood Week."

"Wow," said Eddie, "what a lot of happenings!"

Eddie's Happenings

written and illustrated by
Carolyn Haywood

AN ARCHWAY PAPERBACK
Published by POCKET BOOKS • NEW YORK

An Archway Paperback published by
POCKET BOOKS, a division of Simon & Schuster, Inc.
1230 Avenue of the Americas, New York, N.Y. 10020

ISBN: 0-671-43190-0

First Archway Paperback printing December, 1981

10 9 8 7 6 5 4 3 2 1

AN ARCHWAY PAPERBACK and colophon are
trademarks of Simon & Schuster, Inc.

Printed in the U.S.A.

IL 3+

To
Helen Hooker Roelofs
and
Richard Roelofs, Jr.,
with deep appreciation
of their friendship

Contents

Eddie's Happenings

1

A New Idea for Eddie

EDDIE WILSON sat on the stone wall beside the steps leading to the front door of the school. He was waiting for his friend, Boswell Cary, known to everyone as Boodles. Eddie swung his legs and practiced whistling. He was not a very good whistler.

Suddenly Eddie heard someone whistling inside the door, and he called out, "That you, Bood?" There was no answer.

Eddie looked up and saw the new boy who had joined Eddie's class a few days ago coming out of school. He had the strange name of Tewfik Tully, but he hadn't been in the class a day before everyone was calling him Toothpick. He was tall for his age and very thin, so the name Toothpick suited him very well.

"Hi, Toothpick!" Eddie said.

"Hi, yourself!" answered the boy. "Look, Tookey's my name. That's what they call me at home. Tookey!"

"Okay, Tookey!" said Eddie. Then, seeing that Tookey had a yellow book in his hand, he asked, "What's that book you have?"

"Oh, I just picked it out of the wastebasket. Mrs. Andrews threw it away," said Tookey, sitting down beside Eddie. "It's all about events."

"Events!" Eddie exclaimed. "What do you mean *events?*"

"I don't know," said Tookey. "Take a look." He handed the book to Eddie.

"This is more like a magazine than a book," said Eddie, as he opened it. He flipped over the pages. "Why, this is a calendar," he said. Then he began to read aloud. "National Hot Dog Week, Frozen

2

Potato Month, Peanut Week." Eddie stopped for breath. "Wow!" he exclaimed, looking up at Tookey. "This is terrific!"

"What's so terrific about it?" said Tookey.

"Why, these are celebrations," said Eddie. "These are happenings."

Then Boodles came running down the steps, and Eddie called, "Hey, Boodles! Come see!" Eddie waved the magazine.

"What's that?" Boodles asked, as he sat down.

"Boy! Is this great!" said Eddie.

"What's great?" Boodles asked again.

"This magazine," replied Eddie. "Mrs. Andrews threw it into the wastebasket, and Tookey pulled it out. It's a calendar."

"Well, what's so great about a calendar?" Boodles asked. "My mother has one in every room in the house."

"Not like this!" said Eddie, tapping the page with his finger. "This is valuable property!"

"Oh, you mean junk," said Boodles. Then, speaking to Tookey, he said, "You don't know it yet, but Eddie's the junkman around here."

Eddie went right on reading the calendar. "This calendar has every celebration

3

during the year. We've been missing all kinds of celebrations. I guess you think there's only Christmas and Thanksgiving and Fourth of July.''

''Well, they're good celebrations,'' said Boodles. ''But I can think of a couple of others, like George Washington's birthday.''

''And there's Halloween,'' said Tookey. ''It's the greatest! Mischief night and trick or treat!''

''I sure do love celebrations!'' exclaimed Eddie. ''Now we can celebrate all the time. Almost every day in the week we can celebrate something.''

''Well, not on Saturdays,'' said Boodles.

''Why not?'' Eddie asked.

''Because Saturday's always somebody's birthday,'' Boodles replied.

''What do you mean 'Saturday's always somebody's birthday'?'' Eddie looked puzzled.

''You know, Eddie!'' Boodles answered. ''Saturday's the regular birthday day. Everybody has his birthday party on Saturday. Who wants to celebrate something else and miss a birthday party?''

''But you can always have two celebrations at once,'' said Eddie. ''You never

heard of Fourth of July interfering with anybody's birthday party, did you? They just stick American flags in the ice cream. It's simple."

Tookey's mouth opened wide as he listened to the conversation.

Eddie turned a page. "Now look here!" he said. "I'll bet you never knew that there is a National Pickle Week."

"Pickle Week!" exclaimed Boodles. "How do you celebrate Pickle Week? I guess if somebody had a birthday party during Pickle Week, you'd want pickles sticking out of the ice cream."

Tookey laughed so hard that he almost fell off the wall.

"Boodles!" Eddie exclaimed. "Sometimes you remind me of Anna Patricia Wallace. You both mix things up something awful."

"What do you mean I mix things up!" Boodles shouted. "I'm logical, I am. If you have American flags sticking out of the ice cream on the Fourth of July, you have pickles sticking out of the ice cream when you celebrate Pickle Week. But don't show this calendar to Anna Patricia, because if she gets hold of it, she'll think of something worse than pickles and ice cream."

"Oh, this calendar belongs to Tookey," said Eddie, handing it back to Tookey. "This is real valuable property, Tookey," he added rather sadly. "I forgot to look in the wastebasket today."

"You can have it," said Tookey.

"I can?" Eddie exclaimed.

"Sure!" said Tookey. "I wouldn't know what to do with it."

"Thanks!" said Eddie. "That's great!"

Tookey stood up. "Well, so long," he said. As he turned to leave, he asked Boodles, "Is this Eddie some kind of a nut?"

"No," said Boodles, "he's just enthusiastic. You'll get used to him."

When Tookey had gone, Boodles asked Eddie, "Why do you call him Tookey? I thought his name was Toothpick."

"He says they call him Tookey at home," said Eddie, turning the pages to September. "Now let's see what we can celebrate this month."

The boys' heads were together as they read the calendar. In a few minutes, Boodles said, "Why, Eddie! We'd have to travel all over the country, even all over the world, to celebrate all these happenings."

Eddie ignored this remark, and said,

"Oh, boy! Here's a Roundup in Idaho!"

"Well, we don't live in Idaho," said Boodles.

"And a Fair and Rodeo," Eddie went on.

"Where's that?" Boodles asked.

"In Texas," Eddie replied. "I wish I were in Texas!"

"Well, you're not," said Boodles. "If we're going to do any celebrating, we'll have to find something to celebrate right here."

Eddie ran his finger down the list, and in a moment he read out, "Fall Cleanup Time."

"That's no celebration," said Boodles, very forcefully. "That's just a lot of hard work."

"That depends," said Eddie.

"On what?" Boodles asked.

"On who does the hard work," Eddie answered. "If we can get everybody excited about throwing things out, we might find a lot of good stuff."

"You mean you might find a lot of junk for your junk pile," said Boodles.

"My valuable property," said Eddie.

"It's junk," said Boodles, "and I'm not going to help you celebrate Junk Week!"

"Well, look!" said Eddie. "Here's Granddad's Day!"

"I never heard of Granddad's Day," said Boodles. "There's Mother's Day and Father's Day, but I never heard of Granddad's Day."

"Poor Granddad!" said Eddie. "He's been having a day all the time, and he never knew it. Now I guess all the Granddads will be glad to know that they have a day to celebrate."

Suddenly Boodles shouted, "Look at this, Eddie! This whole month is National Pancake Month."

"Great!" said Eddie. "I'll tell my mother we have to have pancakes for breakfast every morning this month. We can have double orders to make up for the days we missed."

The boys were so busy reading the calendar that they didn't see Anna Patricia until she was standing in front of them. "What are you reading?" she asked.

Eddie clapped the magazine shut. "Oh, it's nothing," he replied.

"Eddie Wilson," she said, "it is not nothing! How can it be nothing when I can see it in your hand? What is it?"

"It's just a calendar," Eddie said.

"It's a mighty big calendar," said Anna Patricia. "It's a whole magazine. Please, let me see it, Eddie."

Eddie looked at Boodles and Boodles shrugged his shoulders. "Okay!" said Eddie, handing the magazine to Anna Patricia.

Anna Patricia took it and read the cover aloud. "Calendar of Annual Events. Special Days, Weeks, and Months." Then she asked, "What do you do with it?"

"Celebrate," said Eddie.

"Oh, that's nice," said Anna Patricia. "Let's see what we can celebrate in September."

"It's National Pancake Month," said Boodles.

"Oh!" said Anna Patricia. "Well, how can you celebrate that?"

"By eating pancakes, stupid," said Eddie.

"And there's Granddad's Day," said Boodles. "I bet you didn't know about that!"

Anna Patricia turned the pages until she found the month of September. Then she said, "Here's an Indian Powwow. Let's celebrate that."

Eddie got up and looked over Anna Pa-

tricia's shoulder. "It's in Oklahoma," he said. "We don't live in Oklahoma."

"There are an awful lot of Independence Days," said Anna Patricia. "You could go all over the world celebrating Independence Days."

"That's right!" Eddie agreed. "I guess everybody all over the world had to get away from somebody, and when they got away they shot off a lot of fireworks and said, 'This is Independence Day!' "

"Oh!" Anna Patricia cried out. "Here's Fall Millinery Week! Now that's nice."

"I think this one is better," said Boodles, turning the page. "Pizza Festival Time."

"That's next month," said Eddie. "Don't you see it's next month?"

"Well, I can hardly wait," said Boodles. "I love pizza!"

Anna Patricia sighed. "I don't see how it can be Pancake Month and Millinery Week and Pizza Festival Time all at once."

"And don't forget Cleanup Week," Boodles interrupted.

"And Granddad's Day," Anna Patricia continued, "and all those Independence Days and Indian Powwows."

Eddie looked at Boodles. "Didn't I tell you Annie Pat would get it all mixed up?"

"Well, it's like this, Anna Patricia," said Boodles. "Take Cleanup Week. That's the week everybody throws out their old hats, and that makes it Millinery Week." Boodles turned to Eddie. "Right, Eddie?"

"Right!" Eddie agreed.

"You're both crazy!" said Anna Patricia. "You and Eddie can eat pancakes and pizzas the whole month of September, but I won't."

Boodles pointed to the bottom of the page. "Here's National Tie Week. It says 'to introduce the best tie man of the year.' What do you think of that?"

"I think that's going to be my granddad," said Anna Patricia, handing the calendar back to Eddie. "Good-bye! I'm going to buy my granddad's tie." Anna Patricia walked away.

Boodles said, "I don't know, Eddie. Maybe there *are* too many things to celebrate. I get a little mixed up."

"You would!" said Eddie. "That girl Annie Pat can mix up anybody. What we need to do is make out our own list, and at the top we can put Cleanup Week."

"You would!" exclaimed Boodles, getting up. "Well, Eddie, go ahead and celebrate. I'm going to ride my bike."

"You'll help me. I know you will," Eddie called after him. Then he got up to go home. "And so will Annie Pat," he said to himself, "because she never misses anything."

2

A What-a-Day

THE FOLLOWING morning Eddie brought
the calendar to school. Mrs. Andrews was
busy writing on the blackboard. Eddie
placed the calendar on his desk and opened
it. When Mrs. Andrews turned and saw
Eddie, she said, "Oh, I see you found that
calendar, Eddie. It's full of interesting information, isn't it?"

"Oh, yes!" replied Eddie. "Tookey gave it to me. Why did you throw it away?"

"I have another copy," Mrs. Andrews answered.

"All these days to celebrate! I never knew you could celebrate so much," said Eddie. "Why, if I didn't have to come to school, I could celebrate something every day."

Mrs. Andrews laughed. "Oh, Eddie! I'm glad you have to come to school. We'd miss you very much if you didn't come."

"Well, school would be a lot more fun if we had more celebrations," said Eddie.

"That's right!" said the children, who had gathered around Eddie to look at the calendar. "We want to celebrate! Can't we celebrate?"

"Be quiet," said Mrs. Andrews, "or we'll all be celebrating Hush Day!" The children laughed, and Mrs. Andrews laughed too. Then she said, "I guess you think there isn't any such thing as Hush Day, but there is. It's the day you play silent records on the record player." The children laughed again.

"Don't let's celebrate Hush Day today," said Anna Patricia. "That wouldn't be any fun. There must be something better to celebrate.''

"Look in the book, Eddie," said Mrs. Andrews. "If there is anything to celebrate today, we'll celebrate."

"Get the right page," said Boodles.

"Okay!" said Eddie. "Here's September, and here's Fall Cleanup Week."

"No!" cried the children all together. "No cleanup!"

"Well," said Eddie, "there's Boy Scouts of America Week."

"We're not Boy Scouts," said Rodney. "We're Cub Scouts."

"What about the Bean Soup Celebration?" Boodles asked. "It says it right here." Boodles pointed to the page.

"That won't do," said Eddie. "Where would we get the beans?"

"And how could we make bean soup?" Anna Patricia asked.

"It was just an idea," said Boodles. "I like bean soup."

At that moment Tewfik sauntered into the room. "Hello, Toothpick!" several of the children called to him.

"His name isn't Toothpick," said Eddie. "He's called Tookey."

"Mrs. Andrews calls him Toothpick," said Anna Patricia.

"No," said Mrs. Andrews, "I call him Tewfik, but hereafter I think I'll call him Tookey, too."

Tookey grinned at Mrs. Andrews and walked across the room to join the children who were gathered around Eddie. "What's going on?" Tookey asked.

"Mrs. Andrews says we can celebrate something today," said a girl named Sylvia.

"But we don't know what to celebrate," said Rodney.

"Do you mean it, Mrs. Andrews?" Tookey asked.

"Yes," said Mrs. Andrews, "but you'll have to make up your minds soon, before the bell rings."

"I'm glad I changed to this school," said Tookey. "That other school where I used to go was all spit and polish."

"What's spit and polish?" Anna Patricia asked.

"Oh, that's what they say in the Army," said Tookey. "It means you work all the time. My brother's in the Army, but he's a general so he doesn't have to spit and polish."

18

"He's a general?" said Eddie. "Wow!"

Mrs. Andrews spoke up. "Don't think you're not going to work in this school, Tookey," she said. "There will be plenty of spit and polish."

The children laughed, and Eddie said, "That sounds like another name for Cleanup Week."

"Hurry up, Eddie!" said Anna Patricia. "We have to decide before the bell rings."

"Well, here's National Dog Week," said Eddie. "That would be good to celebrate."

"I don't have a dog," said Anna Patricia. "I can't celebrate Dog Week when I don't have a dog."

"That's ridiculous!" said Eddie. "Anybody who knows what a dog is can celebrate Dog Week. You know what a dog is, don't you?"

"Of course, I know what a dog is," Anna Patricia replied. "Do you think I'm stupid? All I mean is, I don't have a dog that's having a birthday."

"Annie Pat," said Eddie, "you're all mixed up. This celebration hasn't anything to do with birthdays."

"Well then," said Anna Patricia, "what

is there to celebrate about a dog if he doesn't have a birthday?''

"There's lots of things," said Eddie, waving his arms around. "You talk about dogs, what kinds of dogs there are, people tell true stories about dogs. The celebration is all very doggie.''

"Oh!" said Anna Patricia.

"I don't like dogs," said Sylvia. "They bite.''

"Nice dogs don't bite," said Boodles. "If you're nice to dogs, dogs will be nice to you. Never rush at a dog. Then he'll be okay.''

"Rush at them?" said Sylvia. "I never rush at them. They rush at me. I don't think it's fair to celebrate for dogs if we don't celebrate for cats. I love cats, and I have a beautiful Persian cat named Pinkie.''

"Well, it's not Cat Week," said Eddie. "It's Dog Week.''

"How about celebrating Dog and Cat Week," said Anna Patricia.

"Yes, yes!" said some of the children.

Eddie looked at Anna Patricia, and said, "Now you want to bring cats into it. That's just like you, Annie Pat. You're getting this all mixed up."

"Didn't I tell you we should have the Bean Soup Celebration," said Boodles. "Then we wouldn't be getting mixed up with all these dogs and cats."

"We need bean soup for the Bean Soup Celebration," said Eddie. "You'll have to get bean soup off your mind, Bood."

"We don't have any cats either," said Boodles. "You said so yourself. What's the difference between not having bean soup and not having dogs and not having cats?"

"It's just all not having," said Anna Patricia.

Mrs. Andrews interrupted. "This discussion is getting very noisy." As she spoke, the bell rang for school to begin. "Now, boys and girls," she said, "we'll finish this celebration after lunch."

As Eddie carried the calendar to his seat, he said, "But we haven't decided what we're going to celebrate."

Mrs. Andrews laughed. "With all that talk about dogs and cats it must be Dog and Cat Week," she said.

"But Dog and Cat Week isn't listed in the calendar," said Eddie.

"Never mind about that, Eddie," said Mrs. Andrews. "Dog and Cat Week it seems to be."

Boodles put his head in his hands. "I wanted the Bean Soup Celebration," he said.

"Now," said Mrs. Andrews, "it's time for our spelling lesson."

After the spelling lesson the class moved on to other lessons until the bell rang for lunch. Soon the children were at the cafeteria counter with their trays.

Boodles was at the head of the line. He looked up at the woman behind the counter, and said, "Mrs. Green, what kind of soup have you got today?"

"Bean soup," she replied.

"Oh, boy!" Boodles cried at the top of his voice. "It's Bean Soup Day! It's Bean Soup Day!"

The children behind him took up the cry. "It's Bean Soup Day!"

"Do you want some soup?" Mrs. Green asked Boodles.

"I'll say I do!" said Boodles. "I love bean soup."

As Boodles walked away with his tray a big boy bumped against him. The bowl of soup spilled all over the tray and splashed

23

on Boodles' friend, Rodney. The soup was hot. Rodney jumped and knocked the tray with the bowl out of Boodles' hands. It fell to the floor with a loud crash.

"I'm sorry, Boodles," said Rodney, "but that soup was hot."

"It wasn't your fault, Rodney," said Boodles. "It was that big fellow. He knocked me, and he didn't even say he was sorry."

Boodles picked up the pieces of the bowl and the soiled tray and went to the end of the line. At last he reached the counter again. "I'm sorry," he said to Mrs. Green.

"Well, you should be more careful," said Mrs. Green. "I'll give you another bowl of soup, but the bean soup is all gone. This is vegetable soup now."

With a very sad face, Boodles carried his tray with the vegetable soup to the table where his friends were sitting. As he placed the tray on the table, Rodney said, "I'm glad she gave you another bowl of soup."

"Yes," said Boodles, "but she was all out of bean soup. This is vegetable."

"Oh," said Rodney, "you can have my bean soup, Boodles. I haven't started yet." Rodney pushed his bowl of soup over to Boodles.

"You sure you don't mind?" said Boodles.

"No, I don't mind," Rodney replied. "Soup's soup!"

"Thanks, Rodney," said Boodles. Then he dipped his spoon into the bowl of soup. "Oh, boy! Do I like bean soup!"

When the children returned to their classroom, Boodles called out to Mrs. Andrews, "Guess what, Mrs. Andrews?"

"What?" said Mrs. Andrews.

Suddenly the whole class cried, "It's *Bean Soup Day!*"

Mrs. Andrews laughed. "I hope you had a real celebration."

"Oh, yes!" said Eddie. "It began with Boodles dropping his bowl of bean soup. It sure was a happening."

"But Rodney gave me his," said Boodles.

"It all sounds very jolly!" said Mrs. Andrews.

At the end of the day Eddie left the school with Tookey. As they walked across the school yard, Eddie said, "Did you say your brother is a general in the Army?"

"That's right!" said Tookey.

"How many stars?" Eddie asked.

"What do you mean *stars?*" Tookey replied.

"Well, you know," said Eddie. "Generals have stars. My great grandfather was a two-star general. What's your brother?"

"Oh, my brother has lots of stars," said Tookey. "So long, Eddie!" Tookey ran off.

3

A Smelly Happening

THE NEXT two weeks were so busy for
Mrs. Andrews' class that there wasn't time
to think about celebrations. The calendar
stayed in Eddie's book bag. The children
had to study spelling, history, geography,
math, and there were new books to read.

On Friday Eddie said, "It sure has been
spit and polish this week. We must have
missed a lot of celebrations."

"Well, it may be spit and polish," said Boodles, "but I'll tell you there's an awful stink around here!"

"Boswell Cary!" said Mrs. Andrews. "Can't you find a better word than that?"

"Don't you smell it, Mrs. Andrews?" Boodles asked.

"There *is* something peculiar in the air," said Mrs. Andrews, "but I've sprayed the room every morning with an air deodorant."

"I guess it's pollution," said Eddie. "Every bad odor is pollution, isn't it, Mrs. Andrews?"

"That's right, Eddie," Mrs. Andrews answered. "It probably comes from the buses."

Anna Patricia, who sat on the opposite side of the room from the windows, next to the closet, said, "It's worse over here." She held her nose.

Later in the morning Mrs. Andrews sent Boodles to the closet to get some paper. When he opened the door, he said, "Phew! The stink is terrible in this closet!"

"Close the door quickly," said Mrs. Andrews.

Anna Patricia put her handkerchief to

her nose, and said, "Oh, it's awful! May I change my seat?"

"That's some pollution!" Boodles exclaimed, as he closed the closet door.

"I'll clean out the closet this afternoon after school," said Mrs. Andrews.

"I'll help you," said Eddie. Eddie was always ready to rummage around in closets. Very often he found things that he considered treasures. Either he added them to his store of junk or used them for trading with his friends. The girl next door, Sidney, usually was interested in a trade, for Sidney was also a junk collector.

Anna Patricia's seat was changed, and Mrs. Andrews sprayed the room again. Then the children settled down to their lessons. All day long any child who walked past the closet held his nose. Once Mrs. Andrews opened the closet door to take some paper from one of the shelves. Many of the children said, "Phew!" and held their noses.

"Now it's not as bad as that," said Mrs. Andrews.

"Maybe you have a cold in your head, Mrs. Andrews," said Sylvia.

"I promise you we'll have pure air in

MAKE YOUR READING GROW

this room tomorrow," said Mrs. Andrews, spraying a mist into the air once more.

The children were all glad to leave at the end of the day, but Eddie was delighted to stay behind. He was so anxious to find out what was in the closet that he didn't mind the bad odor.

When Eddie and Mrs. Andrews were alone, she said, "Are you sure you want to help me clean out this closet, Eddie?"

"Oh, sure!" said Eddie.

"Very well!" said Mrs. Andrews, opening the closet door.

"Maybe something died in there," said Eddie, taking a large package of paper from Mrs. Andrews' hands.

"Oh, Eddie! I hope not!" said Mrs. Andrews.

"It would be very interesting," said Eddie, piling the packages of paper on a nearby desk. "Maybe we'll find a skeleton."

"Eddie!" Mrs. Andrews cried. "Will you please stop! Your ideas are awful."

"I don't have any skeletons," said Eddie, "and I sure would like to find one!"

"Well, not in this closet," said Mrs. Andrews, handing Eddie a box of chalk.

"I guess a skeleton wouldn't make this

much of a smell," said Eddie. "Must be some rotten meat around."

"Eddie," Mrs. Andrews cried again, "will you stop it!"

"You can't tell. Somebody may have put a hamburger in there," said Eddie, taking some jars of paste from Mrs. Andrews.

"Now who would put a hamburger in this closet?" Mrs. Andrews asked, climbing on the small stepladder.

"Well, it smells like rotten hamburger to me," said Eddie. "Do you know how I know, Mrs. Andrews?"

Mrs. Andrews made no reply. She was busy moving some jars of poster paint.

"I'll tell you," said Eddie. "A hamburger dropped down behind our refrigerator once and did it make a stink!"

"*Smell* or *odor* is a better word, Eddie," said Mrs. Andrews. Then she screamed, "Oh, oh, oh!" and almost fell off the ladder.

"What is it?" said Eddie.

Mrs. Andrews sat down on the nearest desk that was not piled with supplies from the closet. She pointed to a row of paint jars on the top shelf. One of them did not have any lid. "That jar of paint!" she cried. "There's a dead mouse in it!"

34

"Do you want me to get it?" said Eddie, all excited. "I'll get it."

"Oh, no!" said Mrs. Andrews. "You might drop it. Then it would spill all over the floor. I'll get it."

"Boy, oh boy!" said Eddie. "Wouldn't this be great for Show and Tell!"

"Show and Tell!" Mrs. Andrews cried. "Eddie, how could you think of such a thing!" Mrs. Andrews got up from the desk. "I'll climb up and get it," she said, "and when I hand it down to you, whatever you do don't drop it."

"I won't drop it," said Eddie. "I'll be careful."

"I'll see if I can find the lid." Mrs. Andrews reached around on the shelf. "It must be here."

"What color is it?" Eddie asked.

"It's just a tin lid. The lids are white," Mrs. Andrews replied.

"I mean the mouse," said Eddie. "What color is the mouse?"

"Well, it's in the jar of purple paint," said Mrs. Andrews.

"Never mind the lid," said Eddie. "Give me the jar. You can find the lid after you give me the jar."

"Do be careful," said Mrs. Andrews, as

35

Eddie reached up for the jar. "And don't stand there holding it. Put it down."

Eddie didn't put it down. Instead, he stood beside the ladder. "The poor little mouse!" Eddie murmured. "I guess he thought the paint was good to eat. The poor little mouse!"

"Eddie, don't stand there with that terrible jar in your hands," said Mrs. Andrews. "Put it on the floor outside our door until we get all these supplies back in the closet. No, you had better find Mr. Brown, the school maintenance man, and tell him to get rid of it."

"Oh, Mrs. Andrews, can't I keep it for Show and Tell? It's the best Show and Tell I ever had!" Eddie coaxed.

"Eddie," Mrs. Andrews cried, "you cannot keep it for Show and Tell. Of course not! You haven't had Show and Tell since you were in first and second grade."

"I know," said Eddie, "but when I was in first and second grade, I didn't have a purple mouse. Now I have this nifty purple mouse, why can't I have Show and Tell? If you could find the lid, couldn't I? It wouldn't smell if it had a lid," said Eddie.

"Eddie, with or without the lid, you cannot keep it for Show and Tell," said his teacher.

"Too bad," said Eddie. "It would be super! Nobody ever had a purple mouse for Show and Tell."

"Take it out of the room," said Mrs. Andrews, "and see if you can find Mr. Brown."

Eddie carried the jar out of the room. He placed it on the floor beside the door and went down the hall to look for Mr. Brown. He wasn't in any of the empty classrooms. Eddie went to the main door and looked for Mr. Brown. He didn't see him, but he did see Boodles, sitting on the bottom step. "Hi, Bood!" he called. "Come here."

Boodles ran up the steps. "I'm waiting for you," he said. "Are you ready to go home?"

"Oh, Boodles!" said Eddie. "Wait till you see what I've got!"

"What is it?" said Boodles.

"I've got a purple mouse," Eddie replied.

"You're kidding!" said Boodles. "Where?"

"Wait right here," said Eddie. "I'll get it."

Eddie went back and picked up the jar. Then he carried it out to Boodles.

Boodles took the jar and looked in it. "The mouse is dead!" he exclaimed.

"That's right," said Eddie. "That's what made the stink, but it's not so bad out here. You don't smell it so much."

"What are you going to do with it?" Boodles asked.

"I haven't decided," said Eddie. "I want to keep it for Show and Tell, but Mrs. Andrews won't let me." Eddie turned to go back into the school.

Boodles still was holding the jar. "What do you want me to do with it?" he asked.

"Just keep it for me until I finish helping Mrs. Andrews," said Eddie.

"Well, hurry up!" said Boodles.

When Eddie returned, Mrs. Andrews said, "Did you find Mr. Brown?"

"Couldn't find him anywhere," Eddie replied.

"Did you get rid of that terrible jar?" said Mrs. Andrews. "I found the lid."

"Well, I sort of got rid of it," said Eddie.

"What do you mean 'sort of'?" Mrs. Andrews asked.

"Well, ah, well," said Eddie, "I gave it to Boodles."

"You gave it to Boodles!" Mrs. Andrews exclaimed. "What is Boodles going to do with it?"

"He's waiting for me to tell him," said Eddie.

"Eddie, you are the limit!" said Mrs. Andrews, as Eddie began to hand up the packages of paper. "You must get rid of that mouse. It isn't healthy to keep it around. I can't understand why you couldn't find Mr. Brown. The mouse should go into the incinerator."

"I know where the incinerator is," said Eddie. "As soon as we finish here, I'll put the mouse in the incinerator."

"That's good, Eddie. You do that," said Mrs. Andrews.

When all the supplies were back on the shelves of the closet, Mrs. Andrews said, "Thank you for helping me, Eddie. Now we'll go home."

"Oh, it was great!" said Eddie. "Finding that purple mouse was great, wasn't it, Mrs. Andrews?"

"We'll have a lot to tell the children on Monday," said Mrs. Andrews.

Eddie sighed. "Yes," he said, "but it would have been the greatest for Show and Tell. I'll take the lid and put it on the jar."

Eddie walked to Mrs. Andrews' car with her. Then he went back to Boodles. He was sitting on the step with the jar beside him.

When Boodles saw Eddie, he said, "What are you going to do with this mouse?"

"Have to put it in the incinerator," said Eddie.

"Can't you think of anything better than that?" Boodles asked.

Eddie led the way to the door of the basement, where the incinerator stood. He turned the doorknob, but the door was locked.

"Good!" said Boodles. "Now what?"

"I'll have to take it home," said Eddie.

"Home?" said Boodles. "Your mother sure will throw you out!"

"Well, we'll take it to your house," said Eddie.

"My house?" exclaimed Boodles. "Do you want my mother to throw up? My mother's very jumpy."

"I still think it would be great for Show and Tell," said Eddie.

"Not indoors," said Boodles.

Eddie looked at Boodles thoughtfully. "Boodles," said Eddie, "you've given me

41

a great idea. Let's go to my house and bring out a table. We'll set up the table on the sidewalk and have our own show and tell!''

"Sounds great," said Boodles.

The boys walked to their bicycles. Eddie put the lid on the jar and placed it in the wire basket on his bicycle. The boys pedaled over to Eddie's house as fast as they could go. When they arrived, Eddie lifted the jar out of his basket and placed it on the ground. Then he said to Boodles, "There's a little table in the garage. You drag it out front while I make a sign."

"Okay!" said Boodles, opening the garage door.

Eddie went into the house, but he was back soon with the sign. It read *2¢, Show and Tell*. Underneath was, *1¢ for Show*, and *1¢ for Tell*.

In a few minutes Boodles and Eddie were sitting behind the table. The jar stood in front of the sign, which was propped up with a brick. They were ready for customers.

The first person to come by arrived in a red car. He was Eddie's old friend, Mr. Kilpatrick, the policeman. Eddie hadn't seen Mr. Kilpatrick for a long time, because Mr. Kilpatrick no longer took the children across the street near the school. He had been promoted and was a captain now.

Mr. Kilpatrick drew up to the curb, and Eddie called out, "Hi, Mr. Kilpatrick!"

As Mr. Kilpatrick got out of his car, he said, "Well, how is my old friend, Eddie? And sure enough here's Boodles too!"

Mr. Kilpatrick walked to the table. "What's going on?" he asked.

"It's Show and Tell, Mr. Kilpatrick," said Eddie. "We show first and tell afterward."

"That's fair enough," said Mr. Kilpatrick, as he put down a penny. "Now what have you got to show me?"

Eddie lifted the lid, and Mr. Kilpatrick looked into the jar. He quickly drew back and held his nose. "Land of mercy!" he cried. "What is it?"

"It's a purple mouse," said Eddie. "Do you want to hear the Tell part?"

"No thanks," said the policeman. "I got my money's worth on Show."

"Well," said Eddie, "being it's you, I'll tell you the Tell part for nothing."

"Sure, that's mighty generous!" said Mr. Kilpatrick.

Eddie told the whole story while Mr. Kilpatrick stood holding the lid down on the jar.

When Eddie finished, Mr. Kilpatrick said, "Now that's all very interesting, Eddie, but I think I had better take this mouse off and give it a proper funeral."

"Oh, Mr. Kilpatrick," Eddie cried, "you're not going to take it away, are you? We've only made a cent so far."

Mr. Kilpatrick put his hand in his pocket, and said, "Well, here's another one. The Tell part was worth it." He put down the penny and picked up the jar.

As Mr. Kilpatrick turned to walk back to his car, Eddie cried, "Do you have to take it, Mr. Kilpatrick? Do you have to?"

Mr. Kilpatrick looked back, and said, "That I do. Pollution, you know. Pollution!"

4

Tookey Tells a Tale

EDDIE HARDLY could wait until Monday. Although he had nothing to show, he knew he had a good story to tell.

As soon as the bell rang for school to begin, Eddie held up his hand.

"Yes, Eddie!" said Mrs. Andrews.

"May I tell about you know what?" Eddie asked.

"Indeed you can," Mrs. Andrews replied. "I know how anxious the children are to hear what we found in the closet."

Eddie walked to the front of the room and faced the class. "I'm sorry I don't have it to show," he said, "but Mrs. Andrews didn't think it was a good idea for me to keep it."

A groan went up from the class, for they all were certain that anything with such an odor would be exciting to see. The children sat silent as Eddie told the story of the mouse in the jar of paint. He didn't leave anything out. Of course, Mrs. Andrews was interested in the end of the story. She was glad that Mr. Kilpatrick had appeared on the scene.

When Eddie finished, many of the children spoke up. "I'm glad I didn't find that mouse!" said Sylvia.

Sidney pouted. "I think you were mean, Eddie," she said. "What good is it for me to live next door to you, if you don't show me things? I think you were real mean."

"Well, Sid! Mr. Kilpatrick drove off with it before I had a chance to show it to anybody except Boodles," said Eddie.

"What kind of mouse was it?" Anna Patricia asked. "Was it a house mouse or a field mouse?"

"I don't know," Eddie replied.

"Well, I'm glad you don't know," said Anna Patricia, "because if it was a field mouse, I would feel awful. They're so cute."

"Well, it sure made a beaut of a pollute!" said Boodles.

Tookey raised his hand. "Yes, Tookey!" said Mrs. Andrews.

"I have something better than that," he said. "I can't bring it to school to show, though, because my mother won't let me take it out of my room. It's a skull."

"Oh!" cried Sylvia. "I don't want to see that. I don't like skulls. They scare me!"

"Well, Tookey, we must get on with lessons now," said Mrs. Andrews. "You can tell about your skull some other day." Another groan went up from all the children except Sylvia, who wanted nothing to do with skulls.

At lunchtime a crowd of children gathered around Tookey. They all wanted to sit at his table. Eddie and Boodles were in the center of things, Eddie on one side of Tookey and Boodles on the other. "Tell us about the skull, Tookey," Eddie urged.

"It's a goat," said Tookey.

Boodles gasped. Looking around at the

children, whose eyes seemed to be bulging, Tookey said, "It's a mountain goat."

Eddie choked on his soup. When he recovered, he said, "A real mountain goat?"

"If I had been carrying a shovel, I could have had the whole thing," said Tookey. "But still the skull is a very important part of a goat. Specially when it has the horns."

"Boy! Imagine that!" Boodles exclaimed. "It's got horns!"

"All goats have horns," said Tookey. "Any dummy knows that."

"Well, sure," Boodles agreed, "but just think of owning a goat's skull with horns! That would be real valuable property, wouldn't it, Eddie! That wouldn't be junk!"

"Tell us about it, Tookey," said Eddie. "How did you get it? Tell us about it."

"Well," said Tookey, sounding very important, "it was like this. One day I went with my family to visit some relatives. They live in a place near the ocean, where there are a lot of sand dunes. I was playing outside with my little kid cousin, and all of a sudden he said, 'I know where there's a goat.' "

"I said, 'What kind of a goat?' and he said, 'I guess it's a dead goat.' "

Every eye was on Tookey's face. "I said

to the kid, 'Where is it?' and he said, 'I can take you to see it!' So we started off. On the way he said, 'It's buried in the sand.' 'How do you know it's there, if it's buried?' I said. 'The horns are sticking out,' said the kid.''

Tookey looked at his listeners. They had stopped eating. Most of their mouths were open. " 'Well, why didn't you tell me it was buried?' I said. 'We should have brought a shovel.' 'I think you can pull it up,' said my cousin. 'If I were bigger, I betcher I could pull it up. You just get hold of the horns and it will come right up, 'cause you're strong.' ''

The children around the table were breathless. They were hanging on every word that Tookey uttered, and Tookey was enjoying himself. "Well," he continued, "it was a long walk, but finally we came to a very lonely spot, and sure enough sticking out of the sand were two horns.''

"Oh, were you lucky!" said Eddie.

"How's that for valuable property, Eddie?" said Boodles.

"I'll say!" Eddie exclaimed. "What did you do then?"

"What did I do!" said Tookey. "I

grabbed hold of those two horns and pulled, and up came the whole head." Tookey looked around the table, and said, "Yes sir! The whole head of that mountain goat."

"I thought you said it was a skull," said Eddie.

"What's the difference?" Tookey grumbled.

"Well, a skull is just bones," said Eddie.

"That's what it was," said Tookey. "I mean, that's what it is."

Eddie looked at Tookey, and said, "I know a lot about goats. I owned one once. Her name was Gardenia. I finally took her down to my Uncle Ed's ranch in Texas. He raises goats."

"Does he raise mountain goats?" Tookey asked.

"Oh, no!" Eddie replied. "Just regular goats."

At this moment the bell rang. The lunch period was over.

After school Eddie stopped Tookey as they were leaving the school yard. "Say, Tookey!" said Eddie. "Can't you bring that goat's skull to school?"

"I'm not allowed," said Tookey.

"Well, can I come over to your house and see it some time?" Eddie asked.

"Maybe," Tookey replied. "Someday."

Eddie looked at Tookey sharply and said, "Are you sure it's a mountain goat?"

"Course it's a mountain goat," Tookey replied.

"How do you know?" Eddie asked.

Tookey's face got very red, and he snapped, "Because I say so."

"But Tookey," said Eddie, "what would a mountain goat be doing at the seashore?"

Tookey was mad now. "I don't know how it got there," he said. "Maybe it escaped from a zoo or something."

"Maybe," Eddie said, as Tookey ran off. Eddie shook his head. He was puzzled.

Over the next month Tookey said nothing more about the goat's skull. Eddie tried several times to bring up the subject. Once he said, "You know, Tookey, if you took that goat's skull to a museum of natural history, you could find out whether it really is a mountain goat."

"It's a mountain goat all right," said Tookey. "I don't have to take it to any museum."

"I wish I could see it," said Eddie.

"Maybe I'll show it to you someday," said Tookey. "Maybe!"

Some weeks later Tookey invited Eddie and Boodles to his birthday party. The two boys accepted and waited impatiently for the day to come. They both were looking forward to seeing the skull of the goat. Early Saturday afternoon they arrived on their bicycles at the same time. "Now we'll see that goat," said Boodles to Eddie, as they parked their bikes.

"Yes," Eddie replied, "we'll be sure to see it today."

The party was being held in the basement playroom, and Eddie and Boodles could hear the boys and girls belowstairs when Tookey's mother opened the front door. "Go right down," she said, as she led the boys to the basement door.

Boodles and Eddie each had a birthday present for Tookey. When Eddie handed his package to Tookey, he said, "Happy birthday! Can we see the goat's skull?"

"Thanks!" said Tookey to Eddie and Boodles. "Thanks a lot for the presents."

"Can we see it?" Eddie urged Tookey.

"Not today," said Tookey. "I can't show it to you today, because the baby's asleep in my room."

"Maybe the baby will wake up!" said Eddie hopefully.

"Oh, she sleeps all afternoon," said Tookey, as he opened Eddie's present. It was a penknife.

"I'd be real quiet," said Eddie.

"No," said Tookey, "she would cry if you made the littlest sound."

Some time later, while the boys and girls were playing a game, Eddie went up the stairs to the kitchen. Tookey's mother was washing her hands at the kitchen sink. When she saw Eddie, she said, "What can I do for you?"

"I'd like to see the baby," said Eddie.

"Do you like babies?" Mrs. Tully asked.

"Oh, I'm crazy about babies," said Eddie. "I wish we had one at my house. I wish I had a baby sister like Tookey has."

"Just a minute," said Tookey's mother. "I'll get her."

"Oh, I can come with you!" said Eddie.

"No, it's no trouble at all," said Mrs. Tully. "I'll get her. You eat a cookie while I get the baby." She pointed to a plate piled high with cookies.

Eddie helped himself to a cookie and watched Tookey's mother open a door in the hall. In a few minutes she was back with the baby. "She's still asleep," she said, holding the baby low enough for Eddie to see her.

"She's a very nice baby," said Eddie, "but I guess we better put her back in her crib."

Mrs. Tully held the baby close, and said, "Now you run on down to the party while I take her back. You don't want to miss anything."

"I sure don't!" said Eddie to himself, as he went down the stairs.

When he joined the party again, Boodles, who had seen Eddie go up the stairs, whispered to him, "Did you see it? Did you see the goat?"

"No," Eddie replied, "just the baby. But I know it's in the room next to the dining room."

After the children had eaten their ice cream and cookies, Eddie slipped away from the table again and went upstairs. This time no one was in the kitchen. Eddie went out the back door and walked around the side of the house. He peeked into the first window. It opened on the dining room, so Eddie was sure the next window would be in Tookey's bedroom. He went very quietly toward it, so he wouldn't wake the baby. Then Tookey's mother might rush into the room before he had a chance to get a good look around. He hoped the window would be open so that he could stick his head inside.

As he crept toward the window he could see that it *was* open. In a few moments, thought Eddie, he would see the skull of that goat. Everything was working out as Eddie had hoped it would. When he reached the window, he quickly thrust his head forward. Instead of his head going into the room, however, it smacked into the window screen, which he had not noticed. "Ouch!" he cried.

Then he heard a deep voice call, "Who's there?"

To his surprise, Eddie found himself staring into the face of a young man.

"Do you want to scare this baby!" the man asked. "Who are you anyway?"

"I—I'm Eddie!" Eddie stammered.

"Well, Eddie! Your face is dirty," said the man. "You shouldn't go around poking your face into window screens."

"Oh!" said Eddie, rubbing his face with his sleeve.

"Are you part of the birthday party?" the young man asked.

"Yes," said Eddie.

"How's it going?" said the man.

"Oh, fine, fine!" Eddie replied. "How's the baby?"

"She's okay!" said the man.

"Are you the general?" Eddie asked next.

Tookey's brother laughed very hard. "The general!" he exclaimed. "Just now I'm the baby sitter."

"I guess you couldn't show me Tookey's skull, could you?" Eddie asked.

"Skull?" Tookey's brother repeated. "What do you mean *skull?*"

"The goat," said Eddie.

"Oh, the goat!" said Tookey's brother, looking around the room. "I don't see it. Maybe Tookey put it away."

"I sure would like to see it," said Eddie, turning away from the window. He was starting to walk back to the kitchen door when Tookey's brother called him.

Eddie ran to the window and looked in it. "I guess this is it," Tookey's brother said to Eddie. "It was behind the chair. Must have fallen off the wall."

Eddie's heart beat a little faster. At last he was going to see the skull with the horns. But what Tookey's brother was

60

holding up was not a skull. It was a picture of a beautiful goat. Eddie could read the words under the goat. *Rocky Mountain Goat.*

"Thanks!" said Eddie. "It's great!"

When Eddie returned to the party, Boodles whispered, "Did you see it?"

"I just saw a *picture* of a goat," Eddie whispered back.

"No skull with horns?" said Boodles.

"If there is one," Eddie whispered, "it isn't there."

"Oh, that's awful!" said Boodles. "You missed the birthday cake too. It was super!"

At that very moment Tookey's mother called down. "Come, children! It's time to go home."

"What a day!" said Eddie to himself. "I only had half the birthday party, and I didn't see the skull of the goat. This celebration sure was a lemon!"

5

The Sheriff's Badge

FROM TIME to time some child would ask
Tookey about the goat's skull, but after
Tookey's birthday party Eddie never men-
tioned it. Without saying a word, he listened to Tookey's replies—"Maybe someday I'll show it to you," or "Yes, it's
really great! I guess Eddie would like to
have it for his collection."

Several times Boodles said to Eddie,

"Do you think Tookey really has a goat skull with horns after all?"

Each time Eddie gave the same answer, "Maybe he has, but all I saw was a picture of a goat."

"Why don't you tell him about the picture?" said Boodles. "Why don't you say to him that you don't believe he has a goat's skull?"

Eddie looked at Boodles, and said, "Because he'd ask me how come I know about the goat's picture. Then I'd have to say that I sneaked around his house and peeked in his window."

"What of it?" Boodles exclaimed.

"Well, when you think about it," said Eddie, "it's pretty cheeky to go snooping around people's houses."

"Oh, go on!" said Boodles. "The trouble with you, Eddie, is you think too much. Detectives do it all the time. It's the way they solve mysteries, and we have to solve this mystery of Tookey's goat."

"Well, I'm not a snoop!" Eddie replied.

As the weeks passed Eddie and Tookey became good friends. One day Eddie invited Tookey to go home with him and spend the night. The time was set for the following Friday. Friday morning Tookey burst into the classroom before school with his eyes sparkling. He rushed up to Eddie, and said, "Oh, Eddie, have I got something you would like to have! This isn't junk. No sir! Nothing junky about this."

"What is it?" Eddie asked.

"It's my great grandfather's badge! His sheriff's badge! I brought it to show the kids." Then the bell rang, and the children settled at their desks.

Tookey kept looking at the badge in his hand until finally Mrs. Andrews said, "Tookey, whatever you have in your hand, please put it away."

"But I want to tell the class about it," said Tookey.

"Very well," said Mrs. Andrews, "when we finish this geography lesson, you can show it and tell us about it."

Eddie was just as anxious to hear about the sheriff's badge as Tookey was to tell about it. When Mrs. Andrews asked Tookey to come to the front of the class, Eddie was pleased. He hoped Tookey would pass the badge around so that he could look at it carefully. Eddie had seen badges on the sheriffs in Westerns, but he never had held one in his hand. Tookey

had real valuable property this time. He was lucky to have had a great grandfather who had been a sheriff in the Wild West.

Tookey held the badge up for all the children to see. "This," he said, "is my great grandfather's badge. He was a sheriff out in the West when it was real bad, wild country. There were gangs of cowboys who stole each other's horses, and there were Indians who held up stagecoaches and scalped the people. It was terrible."

This information wasn't news to Eddie. He had seen Westerns on television. When would Tookey get on with the part about his great grandfather? he wondered.

"Well now," said Tookey, "I'll pass the badge around." He handed it to Anna Patricia, who was sitting in front of him. Then he continued, "About my grandfather! He only had one eye, 'cause an Indian shot an arrow right through the other one. So he had to wear a black patch over his missing eye, but that didn't keep my great grandfather from being the best shot in the whole bad country. Why, he could shoot from the hip and hit an outlaw's horse right between the eyes. I guess you know what happened to that outlaw!"

"That poor horse!" Anna Patricia called

67

out. "I don't see why he had to shoot the horse!"

Tookey was flushed with excitement as he went on with his story. "Why, I saw him once shoot down five horse thieves. Bang! Bang! Bang!"

Mrs. Andrews interrupted Tookey. "Wait a minute, Tookey," she said. "Did I hear you say *you* saw your great grand-father shoot five horse thieves?"

Tookey's flow of words stopped. Then he stammered, "Well, I-I didn't really see him, but—"

Just at this moment the door opened and a little boy about six years old came into the room. He was carrying a bright red ball.

"Wait, Tookey, until I see what this little boy wants," said Mrs. Andrews.

The boy walked up to Mrs. Andrews. "My mother says the boy who traded me this ball for my great grandfather's sheriff's badge must give it back to me."

The only sound in the room was a little gasp "Oh!" from Sylvia. The rest of the children stared at Tookey. The badge had just reached Eddie's hands. He got up and, because the room was so silent, carried the badge on tiptoe to Mrs. Andrews.

"Thank you, Eddie," said Mrs. Andrews. Then she held it out to the little boy. "Is this the badge?"

The boy smiled at Mrs. Andrews. "Yes, that's it! Thank you! My mother let me bring it to school yesterday for Show and Tell." He handed the red ball to Mrs. Andrews.

When the boy had gone, Mrs. Andrews held the red ball out to Tookey. She looked very severe as she said, "Is this your ball?"

Tookey hung his head. His ears were as bright a red as his ball. Mrs. Andrews put the ball in his hand, and said, "Sit down, Tewfik." She hadn't called him Tewfik for a long time. "We know the whole story now," she said.

Anna Patricia spoke up. "Well," she said, "I certainly am glad that horse didn't get shot through the eye."

"And his great grandfather didn't get shot in the eye by an Indian either," said Boodles.

Some of the children laughed. "Such a story!" Sylvia exclaimed. "I didn't like it anyhow. I've seen much better ones on TV."

"Tookey's got a lot of imagination,

hasn't he, Mrs. Andrews?'' said Rodney. "I thought it was all for real."

"I'm afraid Tookey has an upside-down imagination," said Mrs. Andrews. "Someday he'll have to learn what to do with it."

All the children laughed again except Tookey. "That's funny, Mrs. Andrews!" said Boodles. "An upside-down imagination! That's really funny!"

Tookey slouched in his seat the rest of the morning. His head hung low. Mrs. Andrews didn't ask him to sit up nor did she call on him to answer any questions.

At lunchtime Tookey sat alone. He ate his sandwich quickly. Then he walked over to where Eddie was eating his lunch.

Eddie looked up, and said, "Hi, Tookey! You going home with me to spend the night?"

"I guess so," said Tookey. "You want me to come, don't you?"

"Oh, sure!" said Eddie. "We have to walk home, because I didn't bring my bike."

"Okay," said Tookey, as he walked away.

Boodles called after him, "How's your

upside-down imagination?'' Tookey made no reply.

The afternoon session in Eddie's class was a busy one. The children kept their thoughts on their lessons, and Tookey's story seemed forgotten. Tookey had straightened up. He paid attention to Mrs. Andrews, but he didn't open his mouth all afternoon.

When the bell rang at the end of the day, everyone hurried to leave. They were always in a hurry on Fridays, because the next day was Saturday and would be free for fun.

As Tookey gathered his books together, Mrs. Andrews said, ''Tewfik, I want to speak to you.''

Eddie waited for Tookey at the bottom of the school steps. When he appeared, Eddie just said, ''Hi.''

''Hi,'' Tookey replied, bouncing his red ball.

The boys walked along in silence. Eddie picked up a stick. He whacked the trees with it as they passed under them. Tookey kicked the leaves that lay thick on the sidewalks. Occasionally he bounced his red ball.

Finally Eddie threw the stick away, and said, "Why do you lie?"

"What do you mean *lie?*" Tookey asked. "I don't lie. When my mother asks me if I did something I shouldn't have done, I never lie."

"But Tookey, you make up lies!" said Eddie. "You make up whoppers! Like this morning."

"They're not lies," said Tookey. "I just like to make up things. It's fun."

"Like your brother being a general?" said Eddie. "Your brother isn't a general."

"How do you know?" Tookey asked.

"How old is he?" Eddie questioned.

"He's twenty-two," Tookey replied.

Eddie stood still and laughed. "Tookey, you're nuts!" he said. "He couldn't be a general and only be twenty-two. Nobody is going to believe such crazy talk."

"Well, it's fun to make up stories," said Tookey. "That's not lying. It's just having fun with people. Like my mountain goat."

"What about it?" Eddie asked. At last he was going to hear the truth about the goat. "What about it?"

"Well, my uncle gave me a swell picture

of a mountain goat," said Tookey. "It's a big picture all in color."

"The uncle that lives near the sea-shore?" Eddie asked.

"That's right!" Tookey replied. "Well, that picture hangs on the wall in my room. I look right at it from my bed. Once it fell off the wall, but it didn't break."

Eddie thought to himself, Yes, I know it fell off the wall, but he said nothing.

Tookey continued, "I like to look at that picture, and if I can't go to sleep right away, I think about the goat and I make up stories. You know, things that could happen to it. Real exciting things!"

"Like finding its horns sticking out of the sand?" Eddie asked.

"Well, yes!" Tookey replied.

"And pulling its skull out by the horns?" Eddie added.

"Yeah!" said Tookey.

"So all that skull business is just a great big lie," said Eddie. "You don't have a goat's skull."

Tookey laughed, and said, "No, it's make-believe!" Then he added, "But you won't tell the kids, will you?"

Eddie stood still. Tookey stopped and looked at him. Eddie said, "You've told 'em already, Tookey. Like this morning! You can't fool those kids forever."

"But Eddie, you don't understand," said Tookey. "It's fun to make up stories."

"Sure," Eddie agreed, "but you have to say they're stories and not tell people it's all true. Stories are for books! You're stupid, Tookey! Pretty soon nobody will believe anything you tell 'em. Soon everybody will call you Big-Mouth Tookey!"

That night, after the two boys were in Eddie's bunk beds, Tookey called up from the lower berth. "Eddie, did I ever tell you about my uncle who pitched for one of the major leagues?"

Eddie leaned out of his berth, and said, "Shut up, Tookey, and stop being stupid. Don't you know I'm asleep?"

6

Thanksgiving Game

EDDIE HAD a new football. One day, shortly before Thanksgiving, Eddie was showing it to Boodles and Rodney and Stevie Evans. They were standing together in the school yard.

"Have you ever been to a real football game, Eddie?" Rodney asked, as he handled the football.

"No, I only see the games on TV," Eddie replied.

"It must be great to sit in the grand-stands and root for your team," said Stevie.

"And eat hot dogs and drink pop!" said Boodles.

"And eat peanuts!" said Rodney. "I know they always sell peanuts."

"That's at the circus," said Boodles.

"It's at the football games, too," Rodney insisted. "I can see what's going on when they show the games on TV."

The boys were admiring Eddie's football when Tookey joined the group. "What's going on?" he asked.

"Eddie has a new football, and it's a beaut!" Boodles answered, handing it to Tookey.

"I guess they don't come better than that," said Rodney.

Tookey laughed. "Oh, you should see a real one," he said. "You should see the football my brother plays with. He's the one who's in college. He's a halfback on the varsity."

Boodles poked Eddie in the ribs, and said, "He's not the general, is he, Tookey?"

"Course not!" Tookey replied.

"I guess he plays on a team out in the big bad West," said Boodles.

"Oh yes, the big bad West!" Rodney piped up.

Tookey ignored all the remarks, and said, "He's home now, 'cause he got hurt in one of the games."

"Ain't that too bad!" Boodles sang out, poking Eddie again.

"Why don't you bring his football to school and tell us all about it?" said Stevie.

By now the children had heard many tales about Tookey's family. They had heard of the remarkable things they had done and of the equally remarkable things they owned. Some of the children had begun to think that Tookey lived in a museum, but he never brought anything to show them.

"You seem to have an awful lot of relatives, Tookey," said Eddie. "I never knew anybody with so many uncles and cousins and brothers."

"And great grandfathers!" said Boodles. "Are you sure you only have one mother and one father, Tookey? And what has your baby sister been doing lately?"

"Oh, lay off, Boodles!" said Eddie.

When the boys reached their classroom, Tookey said to Eddie, "What's the matter with those kids? Don't they believe me?"

Eddie looked directly at Tookey, and said, "No, they don't!"

"But it's true!" Tookey retorted. "It's true!"

"That's what you say!" said Eddie.

About a week later Tookey said to Eddie, "My brother's college is playing football here on Thanksgiving."

"How many touchdowns is your brother going to make?" Eddie asked.

"I told you, Eddie. My brother's home, 'cause he got hurt," said Tookey. "He's better now, but he can't play yet. He's going back to college after Thanksgiving."

"You don't say!" said Boodles, who had joined Eddie and Tookey.

"Well, my brother has some tickets for the game," Tookey continued, "and he said he'll take us."

"You mean he's going to take Boodles and me?" said Eddie.

"Yes, and I'm going to ask Rodney and Stevie, too," said Tookey.

"Thanks, Tookey!" said Eddie. "That's great!"

"I'll go tell Rodney and Stevie," said Tookey, running off to find them.

Boodles looked at Eddie, and said, "You mean thanks for nothing!"

81

"Maybe it's true," said Eddie.

"Don't be a dope!" said Boodles. "You know it's always April Fools' Day with Tookey."

At lunchtime Tookey was eating with his four friends. "Now about that Thanksgiving game," he said. "My brother is going to take us in his station wagon. I guess the best place to meet is right here outside the school, because I don't know where you all live. Just be here at eleven o'clock. My brother will take us to lunch before the game."

"Isn't that dandy!" said Boodles, kicking Eddie under the table.

"I'll be sure to wear my earmuffs," said Stevie.

"Bring the football so we can get in the game," said Rodney.

"Why do you say such dumb things?" said Tookey. "I don't know whether to take you or not. Maybe I'll ask somebody else."

"Suit yourself!" said Boodles, as he gathered up his empty plates.

"You don't seem very grateful," said Tookey.

"Sure we are!" Eddie responded. "It's

nice of your brother to ask us to go to the game with him."

On the way back to their classroom, Boodles said to Eddie, "Are you letting Tookey kid you?"

"I think he's telling the truth," said Eddie.

"Eddie, you've got crackers in your head!" said Boodles. "He's just up to one of his tricks. He wants to get us over to school on Thanksgiving, and then he'll let us stand around waiting for something to happen. Well, I'm not coming. He's not going to make a monkey out of me!"

On Thanksgiving Eddie was up early. It was a sunny but chilly morning, good football weather. After Eddie took his bath, he put on a warm pair of slacks and his woolly sweater.

At breakfast, his father said to him, "Well, Eddie, what are your plans for today? You look all spruced up."

"Tookey said his brother is taking a bunch of us to the big college football game," Eddie replied.

"You don't sound too sure," said his father.

"I'm not," Eddie said. "Tookey gets notions."

"Notions?" his father replied. "You mean Tookey builds air castles?"

"Well, something like that. Mrs. Andrews says he's got an upside-down imagination," said Eddie. "But if this football game is an air castle, he better lock himself into it and pull up the drawbridge."

"Where are you meeting?" his father asked.

"Over at school, at eleven o'clock," Eddie answered.

"Shall I drive you over?" his father asked.

"That would be great, Dad!" said Eddie.

A few minutes before eleven o'clock Mr. Wilson drove up to the spot where Tookey said his brother would pick up the boys. No one was around. "Shall I wait with you?" his father asked.

"No thanks, Dad," Eddie replied. "If they don't show up, I'll walk home."

"All right," said his father. "I hope you get to the football game. So long!"

Eddie waved to his father as he drove away. Then he walked up and down in front of the school. Eddie looked up the street, and he looked down the street. He didn't see any of his friends. He watched each car that came near, but none stopped. As he walked up and down, he began to wonder whether Tookey's brother would be the same brother who had showed Eddie the picture of the goat. Eddie hoped he wouldn't say, "Hi, found any goats lately?" Or maybe he would say, "Hi, been peeking into any windows lately?" Then Tookey would ask how Eddie knew his brother.

Eddie began to wish he hadn't come, for now Tookey would know that Eddie had snooped. "Well," said Eddie to himself, "it serves me right!"

It seemed to Eddie that he had been waiting a long time when he saw a green station wagon drive up. There was Tookey on the front seat. A young man Eddie never had seen before was driving. Eddie breathed a sigh of relief.

"Hi, Eddie!" Tookey called out.

Eddie ran to the car. "Hello, Tookey!" he called back.

"Where's everybody?" Tookey asked.

"I don't know," Eddie replied.

Tookey turned to his brother, and said, "Buzz, this is Eddie."

"How are you, Eddie?" said Tookey's brother. "Just call me Buzz! Everybody does."

"It's funny the rest of the gang isn't here," said Tookey.

Tookey's brother shut off the engine, and said, "They'll be along. We'll just wait for them."

Eddie climbed into the car beside Tookey, and he said to Buzz, "It sure is nice of you to take us to the game."

"It's going to be fun for me," Buzz replied, "and I'm glad to meet Tookey's friends."

The longer they waited, the more Eddie began to feel that Buzz was not going to meet any more of Tookey's friends. Every once in a while Buzz looked at his watch. Finally he said, "They couldn't have understood you, Tookey."

"But I told 'em we would pick 'em up right here, didn't I, Eddie?"

"Yepper!" Eddie replied.

"Tookey, I think you've messed it up," his brother said. "Now what am I going to do with all these tickets?"

Eddie spoke up. "I know where the other boys live. We can drive there and find out what happened. Maybe they're sick or something."

"Three sick boys on Thanksgiving Day!" exclaimed Buzz. "That would be a bit unusual, but maybe they all ate green apples! Carry on, Eddie! Lead the way!"

Eddie gave Buzz the directions for reaching Boodles' house. Eddie wondered what Boodles would be doing, and he wasn't surprised when Boodles' mother opened the front door. "Boswell's in the basement washing the dog. Go right down," she said.

As the two boys clattered down the basement stairs, Tookey called out, "Hey, Boodles! What are you doing washing the dog on Thanksgiving? We're ready to go to the game."

Boodles was so surprised that he let go of the dog, and the dog jumped out of the tub. With water and soapsuds flying, he ran to the steps just as Eddie and Tookey reached the bottom. "Catch him! Catch him!" Boodles cried.

The dog ran from the boys, and Boodles and Eddie and Tookey began to chase him around the basement. Soon he was cornered, and Boodles picked him up and put him back into the tub.

"Boodles," Tookey cried, "don't you know that my brother is waiting outside? What's the matter with you?"

"Well, why didn't you say so!" Boodles replied. "Soon as I rinse Laddie off, I'll be right out."

Laddie received a quick rinse. Then he shook himself, flinging water all over the boys. First Boodles rubbed him with a towel. Next he had to change his clothes. From time to time Tookey's brother blew the horn on the car. Finally the three boys appeared. They climbed into the back of the station wagon, and Eddie gave the directions for reaching Rodney's house.

When they arrived, the boys went to the front door and Eddie pushed the bell. In a moment they heard Rodney's voice calling, "Come in! Come in!"

Eddie pushed open the door. A delicious odor of chocolate greeted the boys as they walked into the hall.

"Come on back!" Rodney called. "I'm in the kitchen."

The boys made their way to the kitchen, where the odor of roasting turkey filled the

air. Rodney was at the kitchen stove. "Hi, fellows!" said Rodney.

"Rod!" Tookey called out. "What are you doing?"

"Making fudge!" Rodney replied.

"Fudge!" exclaimed Tookey. "What a thing to be doing on Thanksgiving! Didn't I tell you to meet us at the school? Don't you remember? My brother's taking us to the football game!"

"He is?" said Rodney, beating the fudge. "No kidding?"

"He's sitting outside in the car this minute," said Tookey. "What in thunder are you doing making fudge?"

"I like fudge," Rodney replied.

"Well, will you quit it and get ready to go to the game?" Tookey yelled. "You've got chocolate all over your face."

"Okay," said Rodney, "you beat the fudge, and I'll wash my face and hands."

Tookey took over the fudge. As he beat it, he said, "I don't know what's the matter with you kids! I just don't know!"

Soon there were four boys in the back of the car. As Buzz started off again, he said, "I'm glad we have to get only one more of your friends, Tookey!"

It wasn't far to Stevie's home. The house was built in an apple orchard. As the car stopped in the driveway, the boys heard Stevie call out, "Hi, fellas!"

The boys looked around, but they didn't see Stevie. Then he called again, "I'm here. Up in the tree house."

Tookey ran to the foot of the tree and yelled up to Stevie, "What are you doing up there?"

"Eating an apple," Stevie replied. "Come on up."

Tookey yelled again, "We've come to take you to the game!"

"You have?" Stevie called back. "You mean the football game?"

"Well, what else!" Tookey replied. "Didn't I tell you we were going to the game? What's the matter with you? Didn't you believe me?"

Stevie climbed down from the tree house. A few apples were still lying on the ground. Stevie picked up three apples and handed one to each of the boys. When he handed the apple to Tookey, he said, "No, Took! I didn't believe you, but now I'll go wash my hands." Stevie ran into the house.

Standing under the apple tree, Tookey took a bite out of his apple. He crunched it up. Then he said to Rodney, "Didn't you believe me, Rodney?"

"No, I didn't," Rodney replied, spitting out some seeds.

"And didn't you believe me, Boodles?" Tookey asked.

"Nope!" Boodles replied through a mouthful of apple.

"Well, Eddie believed me, didn't you, Eddie?" said Tookey.

Eddie tossed away the core of his apple.

"Didn't you, Eddie?" Tookey repeated.

Eddie spit out a seed. Then he said, "I was so anxious to go to a football game that I kept telling myself over and over it had to be true! This time it had to be true!"

The horn sounded once again loud and long. It brought Stevie running from the house buttoning his coat. In a few moments all the boys were in the station wagon. Buzz stepped on the accelerator and called back, "I have never had such a hard time getting a crowd to go to a football game! It's too late now to take you to lunch. I'll have to drive right to the field."

"We can get hot dogs there, can't we?" Tookey asked.

"And pop?" said Eddie.

"And peanuts?" said Boodles.

"And maybe Popsicles!" said Rodney.

"It's too cold for Popsicles," Tookey's brother replied, "but you won't go hungry." Then he said to Tookey, "I can't understand what was the matter with these friends of yours, Took!"

"Oh, they just wanted to be sure that I meant it," Tookey replied.

"Humph!" said his brother. "You've been up to your old tricks I'll bet! Maybe this will teach you a lesson."

Buzz pushed the five boys through the gate of the stadium just as the whistle blew for the game to begin.

"Wow!" said Eddie. "I'm really here!" Then he said to Buzz, "I sure hope your team wins! I'll root when you root. Then I won't root for the wrong team. Right, Buzz?"

"Right!" said Buzz.

7

Christmas Is Coming

ONE MORNING in December Eddie pulled a piece of paper out of his pocket. It was his list of celebrations. "Look," he said to Boodles, "we haven't done much celebrating, and this year is almost over. The trouble is nobody likes to celebrate as much as I do."

"We're going to have a big one soon," said Boodles. "The biggest one of the whole year—*Christmas*—and I haven't bought my mother a Christmas present yet.''

"I just have to get one more present," said Eddie. "There's a new little kid who moved in across the street from us. He fell out of bed the other night and broke his arm. I'm going to buy him a toy horse and wagon, 'cause he's crazy about horses. His name is Georgie."

Boodles looked at the list of celebrations that Eddie was holding in his hand. "That's good, Eddie!" he said. "If you buy the little kid a toy, you'll be celebrating Be Kind to Somebody Week! Then you can cross that one off your list."

Eddie laughed. "It'll be a two-in-one celebration."

"I'm going to buy my mother a bird," said Boodles.

"What kind of a bird?" Eddie asked.

"She says either a parakeet or a canary," Boodles replied. "But I haven't saved up enough money yet."

"It's getting pretty close to Christmas," said Eddie.

"I know," said Boodles. "Soon as I get the money, will you go with me to get the bird?"

"Sure," Eddie replied, "I'd like to."

The days went by very quickly, and before long it was the day before Christmas. The schools had closed for the holidays. Suddenly, in the middle of the afternoon, Eddie remembered that he had not bought the horse and wagon for little Georgie. While he was counting the money that he had saved, the telephone rang. Eddie ran to it and picked up the receiver. It was Boodles.

"Say, Eddie!" Boodles shouted into the telephone. "You promised to go with me to buy the bird for my mother's Christmas present. It's almost Christmas eve!"

"Have you got the money?" Eddie asked.

"Yepper!" Boodles replied. "My father gave me some. How about if we go now?"

"Okay!" said Eddie. "I have to buy the toy horse and wagon, too. I'll ask my mother."

In a few minutes Eddie was back at the telephone. "Hey, Bood," he said, "my dad just came in. He says he has to go to town to get some Christmas lights, so we can go with him. We'll pick you up in about fifteen minutes."

"That's great!" said Boodles.

About four o'clock Eddie and his father stopped at Boodles' house. Boodles came out and jumped into the car. As Mr. Wilson drove, he said to the boys, "Now I'll let you out at the pet shop, where Boodles can get his bird. Then you can walk down the street to the department store, where Eddie can get the toy for Georgie. When you come out of the store, wait for me on the curb. I'll pick you up there."

"Okay, Dad!" said Eddie.

Mr. Wilson drove up in front of the pet shop, and the boys got out of the car. "See you later!" said Mr. Wilson, and he drove off.

Eddie and Boodles went into the store. There were a lot of people and a lot of noise from children and puppies. Everyone seemed to be busy selecting puppies or kittens. Eddie and Boodles made their way to the back of the store, where the birds were lined up in their cages. The boys looked them over.

"I don't know whether to get a parakeet or a canary," said Boodles.

"You have to make up your mind quick," said Eddie, " 'cause it's almost Christmas eve and the stores will close soon."

A salesman came up to the boys, and said, "Are you interested in a bird?"

"Yes!" Boodles replied. "It's for my mother for Christmas."

"Do you want a parakeet or a canary?" the man asked.

"Which is the best?" Boodles asked.

"They're both nice birds," the man replied, "but they're different. Parakeets talk and canaries sing. It just depends whether you want a talker or a singer."

"Let me hear one talk," said Boodles.

"Oh, you have to teach them to talk," said the man.

"Well then, I guess I better hear a canary sing," said Boodles.

"My dear boy," said the salesman, "these are not mechanical birds. You have to wait until the bird *wants* to sing."

"But what if it never wanted to sing," said Boodles, looking at the canary in a cage that the man was holding. "Couldn't you make it sing a little bit?"

"No, I can't," said the man, "but I'm sure this canary will sing when it gets into your home. It will be happy, and then it will sing."

"Well, okay!" said Boodles. "I'll take the canary." He put his hand into his

pocket, and said, "I hope I have enough money." Boodles counted out his money. "Is that enough?"

"You'll need another dollar," said the man.

"I haven't got another dollar," Boodles replied.

"Well, the canary and the cage cost a dollar more than you have here," said the salesman.

Boodles' face fell. He let out a big sigh. "It's almost Christmas eve," he said, "and I have to find a bird for my mother." He looked at Eddie. "What am I going to do?"

"Here," said Eddie, fishing into his pocket, "I've got two dollars and fifty cents for the horse and wagon. You take a dollar of it, and I'll see what I can buy for Georgie for a dollar and a half."

"Oh, thanks, Eddie! That's great of you," said Boodles, cheering up. "I'll pay you back."

"I'll put a cover over the cage," said the salesman, as he took Eddie's dollar bill.

Soon the man was back with the cage. He had covered it with a cloth. "Here's your bird," he said. "Take good care of it. Carry it carefully."

"I'll be careful," said Boodles, as he took the cage.

When the boys left the shop, they started to walk down the street to the big department store. Boodles was carrying the cage as carefully as he would have carried an egg on a spoon.

"Say, Boodles!" Eddie complained. "If you're going to poke along like that, the store will be closed before we get there."

"I don't want to jiggle the canary," said Boodles.

"Well, I'll have to get along," said Eddie, "or I won't be able to buy the horse and wagon for Georgie."

"Okay, go on!" said Boodles. "I'll find you upstairs on the toy floor."

Eddie set off at a run. In a few minutes he reached the store. As he went in through the revolving door a man standing inside stopped him. "Merry Christmas, son!" he said to Eddie, laying his hand on Eddie's shoulder. The man was wearing a uniform, and Eddie thought he was a policeman.

"Merry Christmas!" Eddie replied, trying to escape from the man's grasp.

"Son!" said the man. "You have just won a prize!"

"A prize!" said Eddie. "What for?"

"The store is giving a prize to the ten thousandth child to come through that door," the man replied. "You are the one!"

Eddie's mouth fell wide open in surprise. When he closed it, he said, "What's the prize?"

"You will have to go to the toy department," the man replied. "There you will receive the prize from Santa Claus." The man then handed Eddie a Christmas wreath. There was a ribbon tied across the wreath. In large letters it said, *The Winner!* "Just take this wreath to Santa," the man said. "He will give you the prize."

Eddie took the wreath, and said, "Thanks!" He thought he must be dreaming. Hundreds of other people who were doing their last-minute shopping were rushing into the store. But he was the winner, carrying a large wreath! He felt like a jockey who had won a horse race! As Eddie walked to the escalator, he saw people smiling at him. They stood below and watched him as the stairs carried him up to the second floor. Some called out, "Congratulations!" "Good for you!" "Lucky boy!" Eddie began to feel his face turning red.

His face turned redder when he found that he had to stand in a line of little children, who were waiting to speak to Santa Claus. Eddie looked them over. There wasn't a child over four years old. He felt like a giant and wished he hadn't won the prize. Then he thought of Boodles crawling along with the canary. He hoped the store would be closed before Boodles arrived. Why hadn't he told Boodles to wait for him outside?

The line was moving slowly. "Why do these little kids have to say so much to Santa Claus?" Eddie said to himself. By this time, almost Christmas eve, Santa Claus must be sick of listening to them. Eddie looked at Santa Claus. There he sits! he thought. Big as all outdoors! Taking these babies on his knee. Giving out with Ho, ho, ho! Then, to Eddie's horror, he saw Boodles. Boodles was looking all around for him. Eddie wished he could fall through the floor. He looked the other way, but Boodles spotted him.

"Eddie," Boodles shouted, "for cryin' out loud! Are you waiting to sit on Santa Claus's knee?" Boodles began to laugh. He laughed so hard that he doubled over and had to put the birdcage on the floor.

"Shut up, you idiot!" said Eddie. "I've won a prize."

"What for?" said Boodles, sobering up.

"For coming through the front door at the right time," Eddie answered, holding up the wreath.

"Creepers!" said Boodles. "What are you going to get?"

"I don't know," Eddie replied.

"Look, Eddie," said Boodles, "why don't you hold that wreath above your head? Maybe Jolly Old Saint Nick up there will see it and call you up to him."

"Don't know why I didn't think of it," said Eddie, lifting the wreath high above his head. Boodles' suggestion worked. Santa Claus called out, "Why, here's the winner! The winner is here! Come right up!"

Eddie was glad to leave the little children and walk up to Santa Claus. Santa Claus shook Eddie's hand, and said, "My congratulations! I hope you'll like your prize. It is a pleasure for me to give you this beautiful, big rocking horse!"

Eddie as well as Boodles, who had come near, looked at the rocking horse. It was indeed a fine rocking horse, but when Santa Claus asked Eddie to get on it, Eddie's ears turned bright red. "Get on! Get on, son!" said Santa Claus. "See what a fine rocking horse it is!"

Eddie threw his leg over the horse, but his feet wouldn't clear the floor. Santa Claus began to rock the horse, so Eddie had to lift his feet and hold them straight out.

Boodles was trying not to laugh, but he couldn't help himself. He ran behind a pillar and leaned against it, rocking with laughter. When he had laughed himself into hiccups, he came back to Eddie, who was waiting. "What are you going to do with this rocking horse?" Boodles asked.

"I'm going to give it to little Georgie," Eddie replied. "I'm saving a dollar and a half, and I bet this will be Georgie's favorite Christmas present."

"That's a swell idea!" said Boodles. "Is the store going to deliver it for you?"

"No, it's too late," Eddie replied. "I have to take it."

"Do you think you can carry it?" Boodles asked. "It's awful big."

"Oh, sure!" said Eddie.

"Do you want it wrapped?" one of the salesmen asked.

"No, thanks!" Eddie replied. "I can carry it better if it isn't wrapped up."

Eddie still had the wreath, so he hung it around the horse's neck. Then he picked up the burden. First he tried to carry it by the head and the tail, but the rockers stuck out in front of him.

"You can't carry it that way!" said Boodles. "You'll poke those rockers into everybody."

Eddie set the rocking horse down and looked at it. He decided that the best way to carry it would be to put his arms around the belly of the horse. When he had it securely in his grasp, the salesman said, "Are you sure you can manage it?"

"Of course!" said Eddie, as he started off with Boodles. The horse's head was across Eddie's shoulder, and the wreath hung down from the horse's neck. The rockers knocked against Eddie's legs.

"You'll never get that thing down the escalator," said Boodles.

"I can't see where I'm going," said Eddie, "but if you get me to the escalator, I'll be okay."

Boodles, with his birdcage in one hand, guided Eddie with the other. When they reached the head of the escalator, Boodles said, "It's right here, Eddie. Now get on with your right foot. No, I guess you better get on with your left foot."

"What difference does it make!" Eddie cried. "Just tell me where to put my foot. I can't see where to put my foot!"

"Wait until I put the birdcage down," said Boodles. "Then I'll put your foot on the top step." Boodles placed the birdcage on the floor.

Meanwhile, last-minute shoppers were lining up to get on the escalator. "Hurry up!" "Get that thing out of the way!" "You'll break your neck if you try to go down with it!" Those were just a few of the shouts that Eddie could hear.

Suddenly a loud gong rang through the store. It was the closing bell. Now the people behind Eddie shouted louder. "Get out of the way! Do you want us to spend the night here? It's Christmas eve! We'll be locked in!"

Then a young man stepped up to the boys, and said to Eddie, "Look, fella! Let me have that thing. We'll take the elevator."

"I'll meet you down by the front door," said Boodles, as he picked up his birdcage. "I'll go down on the escalator."

Eddie followed the young man to the elevator. When they reached the ground floor, he gave the rocking horse back to Eddie. "I have to go the other way," he said. "Have a merry Christmas!"

"Thanks a lot!" said Eddie. "Merry Christmas to you."

Boodles was waiting by the front door when Eddie came along with the rocking horse. People were hurrying to leave. The revolving door went round and round, carrying them from the warmth of the inside to the cold outside where it had begun to snow.

"Come along!" said Eddie to Boodles, as he moved toward the door. "I can't see very well, so you come in with me."

"Okay!" said Boodles, as he pushed Eddie into one of the sections of the door. "Move in close, Eddie. I can't get the birdcage in."

People were trying to push from behind, so Boodles held the birdcage on top of his head. The door began to move, and when the section that contained Boodles and the birdcage and Eddie and the rocking horse reached the street side, Boodles stepped out. Before Eddie could move, however, someone pushed from behind and Eddie and the rocking horse had to go back into the store. There stood the man who had given the winner's wreath to Eddie. "Sorry, folks," he said, "but I'm locking this door now. Kindly use the side exit."

Eddie had to move off with the rocking horse, followed by a crowd of shoppers. By the time he rounded the corner of the store it was snowing hard. The pavements and streets were white. When Eddie reached Boodles, he said, "Have you seen Dad?"

"I've been so busy looking for you, I haven't been able to look for him," Boodles replied.

The boys pushed through the people to the curb. There was a man selling fresh roasted peanuts. Boodles moved close to the stand. He could feel a little warmth. "I hope this canary doesn't catch cold," said Boodles. "I don't want it to sneeze when I give it to my mother."

"I don't see Dad's car," said Eddie, "but maybe he drove around the block."

"I hope this bird's a singer," said Boodles. Just then there was a sound that Boodles was sure came from inside the cage.

"Eddie!" Boodles cried. "Did you hear that? Did you? This bird's whistling! Do you hear it?"

"That's the peanut roaster, stupid!" said Eddie, as a horn tooted. "There's Dad!"

Eddie and Boodles made their way to the car. When Mr. Wilson saw the rocking horse in Eddie's arms, he got out of the car and came to Eddie. "What have you got there?" he said, in surprise.

"It's a rocking horse for little Georgie," said Eddie. "I won it!"

"Good grief!" said his father, as he loaded it into the back of the car. "Some toy horse and wagon!"

The boys climbed into the front of the car. Boodles held the birdcage on his lap. "Creepers!" said Boodles. "I sure thought I had a whistler for a minute. I hope I've got a singer."

"Oh, sure you have!" said Eddie.

Boodles put his ear to the top of the cage. "It's awful quiet," he said. "You don't think it's dead, do you, Eddie?"

"Course not!" Eddie replied.

"I hope it didn't catch cold while we were standing in the snow," said Boodles.

"Oh, stop worrying, Bood!" said Eddie. "You're driving me nuts!"

"It just made a very funny noise," said Boodles.

"Well then, it's alive," said Eddie.

"I think it sneezed," said Boodles. "Maybe it's got influenza!"

"It's probably just hungry," said Eddie.

When they reached Boodles' house, Boodles got out of the car. Mr. Wilson handed the cage to him. "Thanks, Mr. Wilson!" said Boodles. "Have a merry Christmas!"

Eddie called out, "If you hear that canary whistle again, you'll know it isn't the peanut roaster. Merry Christmas, Boodles! Merry Christmas!"

"Merry Christmas, Eddie!" Boodles replied. "Thanks for being kind to somebody."

When Eddie looked puzzled, Boodles said, "Me! You know! That dollar you loaned me, so that I could buy the bird."

Eddie laughed, and said, "Oh, that! Just a celebration."

8

Washington's Birthday

IT WASN'T very long after New Year's Day that Eddie began to think about the celebrations during the month of February. One morning, in school, Eddie said to his teacher, "February is the shortest month in the year, but it has the most celebrations. Isn't that right, Mrs. Andrews?"

"I guess you *are* right, Eddie," Mrs.

Andrews replied. "There are two important birthdays."

"Abraham Lincoln's and George Washington's," said Rodney.

"Yes," said Mrs. Andrews, writing the two names on the blackboard.

"And Valentine's Day!" said Anna Patricia.

"And Groundhog Day," said Boodles. "That's the day the groundhog comes out. If he sees his shadow, he goes back into the ground and sleeps for six more weeks."

"And there's Pickle Week!" said Eddie.

"Are you sure, Eddie?" said Mrs. Andrews.

"It's in the book," Eddie replied.

Mrs. Andrews added Pickle Week to the list on the blackboard.

"And Chinese New Year's Day," said Johnnie Chan, who was a Chinese boy. "I guess you didn't know about that!"

"And National Negro History Week," said Rodney. "I saw it in Eddie's book."

"There's Pencil Week, too," said Anna Patricia. "And Brotherhood Week. That's to remind us to be just and loving to everybody."

Eddie looked at the list on the blackboard, and said, "Wow, what a lot of happenings!"

"Will we celebrate all of them?" Sylvia asked.

Mrs. Andrews turned from the blackboard. "I'm afraid we wouldn't get anything else done if we celebrated all of these events."

"Washington's Birthday is a national holiday," said Tookey. "I guess we'll celebrate that."

"Indeed, yes!" said Mrs. Andrews. "We have a special reason in this school to celebrate Washington's Birthday."

"Yes," exclaimed Eddie, "and I hope this time our class wins the button."

"Button!" Tookey said. "What button?"

"Tell Tookey about the button, Eddie," said Mrs. Andrews.

"Oh, it's super!" Eddie explained. "Real valuable property! You see, a long time ago somebody gave this school a button that came off George Washington's coat, when he was a general in the Revolutionary War. The person who gave it to the school said that his great, great grandfather was a drummer boy and had served under

117

General Washington when the American Army was at Valley Forge. The button fell off Washington's coat, and his great, great grandfather picked it up. The school keeps it in a glass box."

Rodney held up his hand. "Can I tell the rest?"

"You may," said Mrs. Andrews.

"Well, every year each class does a play about George Washington," said Rodney. "It's not exactly a play, 'cause that would take too long, but it's a little—a little—" Rodney hesitated.

"A happening!" Eddie called out.

"That's it!" said Rodney. "It's a happening. The class that does the best one wins the button. They keep it the whole year until the next February."

"Very good!" said Mrs. Andrews. "It isn't too early to plan what we shall do this February. You must all think about it."

One day, late in January, Tookey said, "Mrs. Andrews, I've been thinking about George Washington's button."

"What about it, Tookey?" Mrs. Andrews asked.

"Don't you think we should decide about our show for Washington's Birthday? I think shows are fun."

Stevie raised his hand. "We could do George Washington chopping down the cherry tree."

"That's silly!" Tookey shouted. "George Washington was a great general. He was the first president of the United States. He was the big boss at the Constitutional Convention, and you want to show him chopping down a cherry tree!"

"He wasn't the 'big boss,' Tookey," said Mrs. Andrews. "He was the Chairman of the Constitutional Convention."

"We could show him crossing the Delaware," said Rodney. "You know, when he went across to fight the redcoats at Trenton."

"No," exclaimed Anna Patricia, "that would leave the girls out. There weren't any girls in the boat."

"There was Molly Pitcher!" said Sylvia. "I could be Molly Pitcher. She even fired a cannon."

"Not in the boat crossing the Delaware," said Anna Patricia.

"That was at the Battle of Monmouth," said Eddie. "I think we should show the camp at Valley Forge."

"No, the fifth grade did that last year," said Sidney. "I remember."

"I think we should do 'Yankee Doodle,' " said Tookey.

Every child in the room looked at Tookey. " 'Yankee Doodle!' " Anna Patricia exclaimed. "That's a song! It doesn't have anything to do with George Washington. It's about *macaroni!*" The children laughed as Anna Patricia recited:

> "Yankee Doodle went to town
> Riding on a pony.
> Stuck a feather in his hat
> And called him macaroni."

"You don't know the one about Washington," said Tookey.

> "And there was Captain Washington
> Upon a slapping stallion
> A giving orders to his men
> I guess there was a million."

Mrs. Andrews said, "Tookey, that is a very original idea, but I'm afraid we couldn't find a 'slapping stallion.' "

"Oh, yes we can!" said Eddie. "We can borrow that horse from the kindergarten. It's a big one. It used to be on a merry-go-round!"

"That idea doesn't sound good to me," said Anna Patricia. "You're leaving out the girls again."

"No," said Tookey, "all the girls can be in it. It says so in the chorus:

"Mind the music and the step
And with the girls be handy."

Eddie raised his hand. "I have a George Washington suit. I could sit on the 'slapping stallion' and give orders to the men."

"Very well, Eddie," said Mrs. Andrews, "you can be George Washington."

"I think it should be pantomime," said Tookey, "except the chorus. The whole class can be the chorus and sing." Tookey sang:

"Yankee Doodle
Keep it up
Yankee Doodle dandy
Mind the music and the step
And with the girls be handy.

Then everybody will dance."

Anna Patricia was grinning from ear to ear. "I think that's fabulous," she said.

"Oh, boy!" Eddie shouted. "This time

we'll win the button, won't we, Mrs. Andrews?''

"Tookey's idea sounds very good," said Mrs. Andrews.

"We could do some other things, too," said Tookey.

"Like what?" Boodles asked.

"Oh, a couple of other mimes, and after each one we could sing the chorus."

"Tell us!" said Eddie.

"There's that part about:

"Fifes and fiddles
And ribbons red as blood
All bound around their middles.

"And then there's:

"I took my hat off, made a bow
And scampered home to mother."

The children laughed so loudly that Mrs. Andrews held up her hand to quiet them, but she laughed too. "Tookey," she said, "that's wonderful. How do you remember all this?"

"It's my favorite song," Tookey replied. "I know a lot about it. The American soldiers sang it as they marched the redcoats to jail.''

''We could do that, Mrs. Andrews,'' said Eddie. ''Some of us could be Americans, and some of us could be British soldiers.''

''We'll have to rehearse,'' said Mrs. Andrews.

When the rehearsals began, all went well, although Tookey complained because George Washington's horse wasn't white. ''When I see George Washington,'' said Tookey, ''I always see him on a white horse.''

''What do you know about that!'' Anna Patricia exclaimed. ''Now Tookey sees George Washington!''

''That's because of his terrific imagination,'' said Sidney.

Eddie turned to Mrs. Andrews, and said, ''Tookey's imagination isn't upside-down this time, is it?''

''No, indeed,'' said Mrs. Andrews, ''and I'm sure Tookey knows now what fun it is to have a right-side-up imagination.''

The George Washington celebration was to take place the day before the holiday. On the morning of the twenty-first of February Mrs. Wilson packed Eddie's George Washington costume in a dark green box and placed the box on a chair beside the front door. When Eddie came down to breakfast, his mother said to him, "I'll drive you to school this morning, because you can't manage that box on your bicycle."

"Oh, thanks!" said Eddie. "That's great!"

When it was time to leave, his mother said, "Eddie, take the box that's on the chair by the front door and put it on the back seat of the car. I'll be out in a few minutes."

"Okay!" said Eddie. He picked up the box and carried it to the car, which was standing in the driveway. It was a dark green car.

On the ground beside one of the back wheels Eddie saw something that shone. He placed the box on the top of the trunk of the car and stooped down to see what the shiny thing could be. He was pleased to find that it was a quarter and added it to the few coins that were in his pocket. Opening the door of the car, he slid under the steering wheel. He settled himself in

the seat and examined the quarter. It had a bit of mud on it. Eddie wiped it off with his handkerchief. He looked at it very carefully to see whether it was a real quarter. By the time his mother got into the car, he had decided that the quarter was not counterfeit.

As Mrs. Wilson turned on the ignition, Eddie said, "Am I lucky! I just picked up a quarter! I guess it's a good omen, finding a piece of money this morning. It probably means our George Washington show will be the greatest and our class will win the button. I'll keep it for a lucky piece."

Mrs. Wilson backed the car out of the driveway, and Eddie was on his way to school.

The first time Mrs. Wilson stopped for a traffic light, the car behind her sounded the horn several times. Mrs. Wilson said to Eddie, "Just listen to that person behind us blowing his horn. Surely he doesn't want me to drive through a red light!" When the light changed, Mrs. Wilson drove on. From time to time someone in a passing car blew his horn as he went by. Eddie's mother grew more annoyed.

At the next stop no horns blew, and the rest of the way to school went quietly.

When Mrs. Wilson stopped the car at the front of the school, Eddie put his hand on the door and said, "You'll be sure to come back this afternoon to see our George Washington show, won't you?"

"Yes, indeed!" his mother replied. "I'll be out all day, but I'll be back in time for the show."

As Eddie opened the door, his mother said, "Don't forget your costume."

Eddie hadn't thought of his costume since he had picked up the quarter. Now he turned around and looked on the back seat of the car. The seat, of course, was empty. "Where is it?" he said.

"What did you do with it?" his mother asked. "You brought it out to the car."

Eddie suddenly felt hot. Beads of perspiration were on his forehead. What had he done with the box! Then he remembered. He had placed the box on the trunk of the car when he had spied the quarter on the ground.

Eddie jumped out of the car and ran to the back. He looked on the lid of the trunk. There was nothing there. His mother climbed out of the car too. "Eddie!" she said. "Where is the box?"

"It's gone!" Eddie cried. "It's gone!"

Then, almost in tears, Eddie told his mother what he had done with the box.

"Well," said his mother, "that explains what all the tooting was about. Those motorists were trying to tell me that there was a box on the back of the car."

"What shall I do?" Eddie moaned. "How can I be George Washington if I don't have my costume?"

"Eddie, it was such a stupid thing to do," said his mother.

"I know!" said Eddie. "That quarter wasn't a lucky piece at all."

"Luck has nothing to do with it," said his mother. "If you keep your wits about you, you won't need lucky pieces. You just have to be smart enough not to be stupid. Now get along or you'll be late."

"What about my costume?" Eddie cried.

"I'll go back and see if I can find out anything about it," his mother replied.

Eddie went into his classroom looking very glum. When he told Mrs. Andrews and the class that he had lost his George Washington costume, everyone groaned. "We won't get the button!" they moaned. "We won't get the prize!"

Eddie was so worried that he had a hard time keeping his mind on his lessons.

Everyone in the class had been so certain that they would have the glass box this year, and now he had spoiled their chances. Tookey's imagination had thought up this wonderful show about "Yankee Doodle," and now, thought Eddie, I've messed it up.

About eleven o'clock the telephone rang in the classroom. Mrs. Andrews picked up the receiver and spoke into the telephone. The children could not hear what Mrs. Andrews was saying, but when she turned around, her face looked very happy. "Eddie," she said, "go to the office. Your costume is there."

"Hurrah!" cried the children, as Eddie left the room.

Eddie ran to the office. There was Mr. Kilpatrick, holding the green box. "Oh, Mr. Kilpatrick!" Eddie cried. "How did you get it?"

"Someone picked it up from the middle of the street and brought it into the police station," Mr. Kilpatrick replied. "A bit later your mother telephoned to ask if the box had been found. When she told me that George Washington's clothes were in it, I was surprised, and when she told me that you were George Washington, I was more surprised." Mr. Kilpatrick handed the box to Eddie.

"Thanks, Mr. Kilpatrick!" said Eddie. "Will you come to our show this afternoon?"

"This is my afternoon off," said Mr. Kilpatrick, "so I'll be glad to come."

Tookey's show was a great success. Eddie rode the "slapping stallion," held up his hand and gave silent orders to his men, and took off his cardboard hat while the children in the class sang "Yankee Doodle" and danced around the stage.

Rodney played a make-believe fife, and Boodles played a fiddle, while Stevie and Dumpty Peterson had "ribbons red as blood all bound around their middles." The redcoats weren't quite certain as to where the jail was, but the Yankees finally pushed them off the stage as the whole school joined Eddie's class in singing "Yankee Doodle." Of course, they were the winners.

Mrs. Andrews let Tookey carry George Washington's button in the glass case back to the classroom. Then there was a great deal of rejoicing.

As Eddie took off his George Washington hat and coat, Tookey said, "You were good, Eddie!"

"Thanks!" Eddie replied. "It was your idea, Tookey. It sure was a great idea!"

Tookey was very quiet. He seemed to be thinking. Then he said, "You know, Eddie! I guess you're right! Stories are for books and plays."

Eddie laughed. Then he said, "You'll write 'em someday, Tookey. Sure as shootin' you'll write 'em."

Tookey looked pleased, and said, "So long, Eddie!"

Eddie found his mother waiting for him in the car. He put the box on the back seat this time before he climbed in beside his mother. "Do you know something, Mother?" Eddie said.

"What?" asked his mother.

"Everybody thought I was George Washington today, but you know who I was, don't you?"

"Who were you?" his mother asked.

"Simple Simon!" Eddie replied. "Today must be Simple Simon's Day." Then Eddie and his mother laughed very, very hard.

"Some happening!" said Eddie.

ABOUT THE AUTHOR
AND ILLUSTRATOR

CAROLYN HAYWOOD is one of the most widely read authors of books for children. Her first story was *"B" is for Betsy,* and she has since written many books, twenty-six of them about her two popular characters Betsy and Eddie. Also available in Archway Paperback editions are *Betsy's Play School, Eddie the Dog Holder, Betsy's Busy Summer, Eddie's Menagerie, Eddie's Green Thumb, Snowbound with Betsy,* and *Betsy's Little Star.*

Miss Haywood was born in Philadelphia, Pennsylvania and studied at the Pennsylvania Academy of Fine Arts. She won the Cresson European Scholarship for distinguished work, and became a portrait painter before she started writing for children. She has illustrated many of her own books.

Miss Haywood now lives in Chestnut Hill, a suburb of Philadelphia.